The Red Sweater

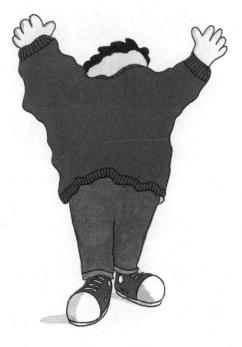

by Peter Maloney
and Felicia Zekauskas

SCHOLASTIC INC.

New York   Toronto   London   Auckland   Sydney
Mexico City   New Delhi   Hong Kong   Buenos Aires

To Betsy Rovegno

SCHOLASTIC and associated logos are trademarks and/or registered trademarks of Scholastic Inc. No part of this publication may be reproduced in whole or in part, or stored in a retrieval system, or transmitted in any form or by any means, electronic, mechanical, photocopying, recording, or otherwise, without written permission of the publisher. For information regarding permission, write to Scholastic Inc., Attention: Permissions Department, 557 Broadway, New York, NY 10012.

ISBN 0-439–39518-6

Library of Congress Cataloging-in-Publication Data available

12 11 10 9 8 7 6 5   4 5 6 7/0

Printed in the U.S.A. • First printing, November 2002 • Book design by Mark Freiman

CHAPTER 1
In School

Peter liked almost everything about school.
He liked learning to read.

He liked learning to count.

And he really liked his teacher,
Mrs. Robinson.

But there was one thing
Peter didn't like
about school—
Russ Deluca.

Chapter 2
Peter's Red Sweater

Peter was the youngest boy in his class. Even though he knew how to dress himself, his mother still set out his clothes every morning.

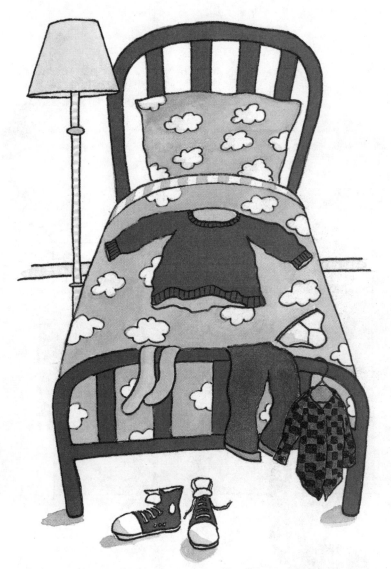

And one thing was always there — his red sweater.

"It will keep you safe," his mother told him. "Cars will stop when they see you."

Peter always looked both ways before he crossed a street. But his red sweater made him feel extra safe.

Of course, there was one thing that Peter's red sweater couldn't protect him from — Russ Deluca.

"Today's the tenth day in a row that you've worn your red sweater," Russ said to Peter. "Don't you have anything else to wear?" Peter didn't say a word.

CHAPTER 3
All Things Red

That afternoon, Mrs. Robinson asked the class to name things that are red.

Felicia raised her hand. "My bow," she said. She pointed to the bright red ribbon in her hair.

"Roses," said Tobi.

"A stop sign," Rich called out.

"Fire engines," said Patty.

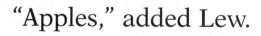
"Apples," added Lew.

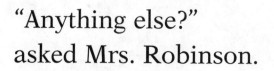
"Anything else?"
asked Mrs. Robinson.

17

"The sweater that Peter wears
every day!" shouted Russ Deluca.

Peter's face turned as red as his sweater.

Chapter 4
Oh No, Not Again!

The next morning, Peter's mother
set out his clothes.
Peter put on his jeans.
He tied his shoelaces.
He tucked in his shirt.

And he walked
to the door.

"Peter," his mother
called out.
"Aren't you forgetting
something?"

"It's too hot for a
sweater," said Peter.
"Too hot!" cried
his mother.
"It's almost November.
Put on your sweater
now."

CHAPTER 5
A Surprise for Peter

Peter put on his red sweater.
He walked very slowly to school.

As he walked, Peter heard *pssst!*
He stopped and looked around.
No one was there.

Then a pretty face with beautiful, bright eyes and a big blue bow popped out of the bushes.

It was Felicia.

"I have an idea," Felicia said.
"Really?" said Peter. "What is it?"
Felicia whispered into Peter's ear.

"Are you sure you don't mind?"
asked Peter.
"Not at all," said Felicia.

The late bell was just about to ring.
Peter and Felicia came running
through the classroom door.

Chapter 6
All's Well That Ends Well

Peter was wearing Felicia's
blue sweater.
Felicia was wearing Peter's
red sweater.

Russ Deluca was so surprised.
His mouth dropped open!

"This sweater is really comfortable,"
whispered Felicia.
"And it will help to protect you
from cars!" Peter smiled.